Jerry's Madness

W.W. Rowe

LARSON PUBLICATIONS
BURDETT, NEW YORK

ISBN-13: 978-1-936012-68-8 | eISBN-13: 978-1-936012-69-5

Publisher's Cataloging-In-Publication Data
(Prepared by The Donohue Group, Inc.)

Rowe, William Woodin.
  Jerry's madness / W.W. Rowe.

    pages : illustrations ; cm -- ([Jerry's M... series])

    Summary: Here at age 11, Jerry has his first kiss, gets steamed over his friends' teasing about it, has a terrifying run-in with a knife-wielding mentally disturbed man, learns more about using The Look for good, sees how we get caught up in what we only imagine is happening, turns an enemy into a friend, helps his team beat their rivals, develops telepathy, and struggles with a bullying conflict that pushes a good friend to see suicide as his only escape.
  Series supplied by publisher.
  Sequel to: Jerry's magic.
  Interest age level: 10 and up.
  Issued also as an ebook.
  ISBN-13: 978-1-936012-68-8
  ISBN-10: 1-936012-68-5

    1. Boys--Conduct of life--Juvenile fiction. 2. People with mental disabilities--Juvenile fiction. 3. Bullying--Juvenile fiction.
4. Friendship--Juvenile fiction. 5. Boys--Conduct of life--Fiction.
6. People with mental disabilities--Fiction. 7. Bullying--Fiction.
8. Friendship--Fiction. I. Title.

PZ7.R7953 Jf 2015

[Fic]   2015933219

Front cover art: Brian Keeler
Interior art: Benjamin Slatoff-Burke

Published by Larson Publications
4936 NYS Route 414
Burdett, New York 14818 USA
https://www.larsonpublications.com

25 24 23 22 21 20 19 18 17 16 15
10 9 8 7 6 5 4 3 2 1

Anger is a short madness.
—Horace

The man who is prone to impatience, irritability,
and anger needs meditation even more than
other men. He needs its harmonizing effect on
the whole personality, its pacifying touch on the
darker impulses and passions.
—Paul Brunton

To eradicate anger he should cultivate its
opposite—forgiveness.
—Paul Brunton

All this vast and wonderful universe is in the end
only the play of mind. We are imprisoned in our
own involuntary creation.
—Paul Brunton

On Madness

IF you wonder, "Am I crazy?" then you're *not* crazy—because a *really* crazy person wouldn't wonder.

At least that's what some people say. But it may not be so simple.

If you get angry enough, maybe you're crazy for a little while. And if you don't understand how your anger harms you, maybe that's crazy too.

Because it does! Each time you do something cruel to others, or even think ugly thoughts about them, you create bad karma for yourself. And when they get mad and retaliate, they make bad karma for themselves. Then, if you get angry and retaliate . . . That's madness, isn't it? (Don't know what karma is? You'll find out soon.)

Do you know someone who is really old? So old, they think the young people are all crazy? Well, when they were young, the old people of their day thought *they* were crazy! That's madness too, isn't it?

And if you see a crazy person who, for example, thinks he's Napoleon, and if you laugh, not realizing that your thoughts create your own world—then what is that?

Madness?

Disclaimer

THIS book contains some pretty scary stuff! Are you a coward? I hope not. Do you try to do everything you read about? I hope not. Why? Because we might end up in jail. Both of us.

Just kidding! There is absolutely no reason I could go to jail for writing this book—or you could go to jail for reading it. Unless they catch us.

ONE

DO you remember Jared Shore?

When Jerry was five, his father died fighting in World War II. A man known as Crazy Wilcox used magic tricks to help Jerry get over the sadness. His mother pretended they lived in a big, fancy mansion with servants. That was silly (because they were poor), but her jokes helped too.

When Jerry was seven, he stopped two bank robbers by triggering an alarm button. He also swindled his friends by dealing in "magic objects." They were junk, but at first Jerry believed they might be real.

When Jerry was ten, he paid the money back, but Suzie Steele wouldn't accept it. She still wore her rusty-nail good-luck charm, tied to a string around her neck. She still believed it was real.

Wilcox told Jerry about his Higher Self. He taught him how to meditate. And he taught him The Look, a powerful form of hypnosis. Jerry solemnly promised to use it only for doing good. The Look can make a person do what you say—and not even know it!

Jerry is eleven now, and he's steaming mad. If he was a bull, he'd be snorting and pawing the ground. "Fit to be tied," his father used to say.

Jerry knows that anger is very harmful. Wilcox told him so. But this isn't just about him. It's about Suzie too! That's why he's so mad.

It happened during recess. Jerry used his golden tongue to persuade Suzie to go with him into the shadows behind the gym. He was showing her his new wristwatch. It has a cool luminous dial! He cupped his hand over it to show how the numbers glow.

Suzie leaned closer, squinting. Her blonde curls jiggled. And suddenly it happened. Quick as magic, his lips were touching hers! And she didn't pull away! For a long moment, he felt soft, warm bliss.

"Jerry!" Suzie slapped his cheek, looking shocked.

But Jerry didn't feel the sting at all. Her heart wasn't in the slap. And she hadn't pulled away for several seconds!

"I couldn't help it," said Jerry. "You looked so—" He was interrupted by a muffled cough.

They both froze.

"What was that?" whispered Suzie. "I dunno," said Jerry.

But he was almost sure he'd glimpsed the faded sneaker of Willie Fielder, disappearing around the corner of the gym. Willie was sneaky and sly. Jerry had tangled with him before.

The next morning, when Jerry walked into his sixth-grade classroom, all the kids were hooting and snickering. On the blackboard was a crude cartoon of a shaggy mutt and a poodle. Their stuck-out tongues were touching. Below the mutt were the letters "J.S." Below the poodle, "S.S."

Suzie was hunched over a book, like she was trying to disappear into its pages.

Jerry glanced over at Willie Fielder. Willie's eyes gleamed. His smile was as sweet as a candy angel on a birthday cake.

So it *was* Willie! Jerry saw red. Bright, steaming, neon red.

His first thought was to use The Look—and make Willie eat a handful of dirt. Or make him pull out his hair. But that was only a flash. Jerry knew it was wrong. *Only for doing good*, he had promised Wilcox.

But how could he control his anger? He took ten slow deep breaths. He pictured himself on a grassy meadow, beside a quiet, peaceful pond, with birds singing.

That worked for a minute or two, but then the pond erupted. A huge red monster raised its scaly head . . . and roared.

That's why Jerry is steaming mad right now. He can't handle such anger! After school, he goes straight to see Wilcox.

TWO

JERRY walks quickly through the forest. The sky looks like puffy gray curtains. Fifty percent chance of rain, the paper said. The safest prediction, never more than half wrong.

"Caw! Caw!" A big black crow flaps by overhead. For some reason, its raspy cry makes Jerry think of the word "caution."

Wilcox lives near the junkyard, in a cardboard house. But he isn't sitting in front, like he usually does.

"Hey, Wilcox!"

No answer. That's strange as snake's feet. Wilcox sits outside even when it's windy and cold, and today is mild.

Jerry goes up close, peers inside the cardboard house. Nobody there. "Wilcox!" he calls. "Where are you? I need some—"

A few minutes later, Jerry wakes up. His head hurts like crazy! But he can't move. He's sitting on the ground, arms behind him, tied to a tree with strong, heavy rope.

A blurry man shuffles over. He's bald, with a fuzzy gray beard. His ears stick way out. He's holding a bottle with a black dog and a white dog on it. Looks like whiskey. He grins a hazy, gap-toothed grin.

"What's your name, sonny?"

Jerry tries to focus on the shimmery man. His head is whirling, and it still hurts. "Whuh? Whud'you say?"

"Your name, you little schmuck! What is it?" He sloshes down the bottle, grabs at something hanging from his belt.

"Uh, Jerry. Jerry Shore."

"Dum de dum," the blurry man sings. He's undoing something hanging from his belt. "What's your address, Jerry?"

Jerry hesitates. Maybe he shouldn't tell this weird man where he lives. His mother is alone there.

The man suddenly waves a hunting knife near Jerry's nose. "Your address, schmuck. Now!"

Jerry strains against the ropes. "Wilcox!" he yells. "Where are you?"

The bald man laughs. "Bad news, sonny boy. He's got a bad case of death." He grins his gap-toothed grin, jabs the butt-end of his hunting knife through the air.

"Bopped him a little too hard. Dum de dum."

Jerry is stunned. Wilcox dead! No, it can't be! He closes his eyes. He almost faints.

"How much money your parents got, sonny? They rich?"

Jerry shakes his head. He won't reveal anything more.

The point of the knife pricks Jerry's cheek. "You've got too many fingers, sonny."

"Whuh?" Jerry feels a trickle of warm blood on his face.

"Fingers! Dum de dum. Tell me where you live, or I'll cut one off."

Jerry gapes. The blurry man seems to mean it.

"Well?"

Jerry frantically tries The Look, but he's too dizzy. Everything is swirling. He can't concentrate.

"Last chance, sonny boy!" The man walks behind the tree, grabs Jerry's tied-up hand. "Maybe your mommy and daddy would like to see one." The blade rests gently on one finger. "Might make them more generous."

Jerry takes a deep breath. "Fifty-six Maple Lane."

The bald man grins. "That's better. I'll go visit your parents, see how much they love you. Dum de dum."

He ties Jerry's mouth with a piece of cloth. "Be quiet 'til I get back, hear?" He walks off through the woods.

Jerry shudders. The bald man must be crazy! His mom will call the police right away . . . unless . . . He shudders again.

The man doesn't return. Jerry stretches his neck around, rubs his head against the tree. This makes him even dizzier, but it gets the cloth loose. His mouth is free.

"Wilcox!" he shouts. "Where are you?" He refuses to believe his friend is dead. "Wilcox!"

The junkyard is quiet, except for a few birds. And the rustling of leaves. Jerry desperately tries to think. His head is getting clearer now.

Before long, he thinks up a plan.

The rope is strong and tight. Jerry helplessly waits. Several times he hears forest rustlings that might be the bald man coming back. He nervously gulps. What if it's a wildcat or a bear? What if the man *never* comes back?

But if he does return, it might be even worse! Jerry shudders. He prays and thinks about his plan.

"Caw! Caw!" The sound comes from high in a pine tree. Is it the same crow?

THREE

AFTER what seems like forever, the bald man is back. But he doesn't look pleased. No, not pleased at all.

"Where your parents gone, Jerry? Timbuktu?" He takes a big drink from the bottle he left behind. "I went to your house. Knocked on the doors and windows. Nobody there."

Jerry sighs with relief. His mother was out. She doesn't know. Yet.

"Hey!" the man says. "I see you got your gag loose." He takes another big swig. "Prolly yelled like crazy, dincha? Well, nobody heard you, sonny boy." He grins. "But don't worry. I'm the persistent type. I'll go back to your house a little later. Dum de dum."

Jerry mumbles something.

"What's that? Speak up!"

Jerry mumbles again.

"I can't hear you!" The man walks up close, bends down. He holds the knife in one hand, the bottle in the other.

Jerry stares directly at him. His head is clear enough to use The Look now. Staring deep into the bald man's eyes, he thinks the magic word Wilcox taught him.

"Whoa!" The man reels, stumbling backwards. "I'm so dizzy! What happened?" He drops the bottle and the knife. "Ooaah!" Staggering in circles, he waves his arms for balance. Finally he sits down with a thud.

"You're not dizzy now," says Jerry. But you need to cut these ropes. Right away!"

"Yes, I do," says the man, grabbing his knife.

"Be very careful, so you don't cut me."

"Yes. So I don't cut you." The man's voice is thick and distant now, like he's totally under.

Soon Jerry's free! "Thank you," he says. A wave of relief sweeps over him—and terrible anger. He glares at the man. "Now you need to cut off your own fingers, one by one!"

The man nods. "Yes, of course. One by one. Which hand?"

Jerry sets his jaw. "The left one."

"Yes, the left one. I'll start with my pinkie."

"Wait!" says Jerry. "Stop." What came over him? He's letting Wilcox down! "Forget about your fingers," he says. "Forget all about them."

The man drops the knife. "What fingers?"

16

"Good. Now you need to go South, where it's, uh, warmer."

"South, where it's warmer."

"Yes. And forget you were ever here. Forget my name and where I live. Forget you ever saw me."

"I don't see anybody. Where are you?"

"Good. Walk five miles today. And five every day after that, for a week. That's thirty-five."

"Yes. For a week. Thirty-five."

"Wait. Make that a little more." Jerry doesn't want him too close. Three weeks will be ninety-five, no, a hundred and five miles. It hurts his head to think. "Three weeks."

"Yes. Three weeks."

A wonderful, horrible idea flashes through Jerry's head. Loon Lake is about fifty miles south! For an instant, he pictures the bald man walking deeper and deeper into the lake until he drowns. But that would be murder! "Wait. If you come to a lake, walk around it."

"Yes. Walk around it."

"And if you see a river, look for a bridge."

"Yes. Look for a bridge." He turns to leave.

Jerry is shaking. He's still in shock. "Wait! Where is the man who was here?"

"The old man? Right where I bopped him. Beyond that pile of junk."

Jerry's heart leaps. Wilcox might still be alive! "Now get going!"

"Yes. I'm going. Good-bye."

The man shuffles off toward the South, where it's warmer.

Jerry breathes a sigh of relief. He'll never see the bald man again, that's for sure! He runs to find Wilcox.

FOUR

JERRY sees Wilcox right away. He's sprawled beside a broken table, lying on his side, mouth partly open. There's a big lump just above his faded red headband. One leg is awkwardly bent.

"Wilcox!" Jerry grabs the old man's wrist, tries to find a pulse. It's faint, but there. He's alive!

Jerry finds some old cushions, carefully props up Wilcox's head. He leans down close. He can hear labored breathing. What should he do? Try slapping his face? Run for help? He doesn't want to leave him here, helpless. A wildcat or a bear might come along and—

"Jerry!"

Jerry jumps. Wilcox has opened his eyes. "Are you okay?"

Wilcox groans. "My head . . ." He feels it with both

hands. "I think so. What happened?"

"A bald man knocked you out. He hit me too, and tied me up. But I used The Look. I made him forget and sent him far away."

"Thank you, Jerry. So you have a big lump too?"

"Yeah. But how did he sneak up on you? Your hearing is so good!"

"He didn't. He asked me to help him look for . . . some keys he dropped. When I saw them and bent over to pick them up, something hard hit my head."

"The handle end of his hunting knife," said Jerry. "He knocked me out too. Are you all right?"

"I think so. Good thing you came along . . . and used your head."

Jerry smiles. Wilcox can still joke. He's okay! "I came with a problem. I'm having trouble controlling my temper."

Wilcox nods, gently. "Did you try deep breaths? And visualization?"

"Sure. But it only helped a little. I was really mad. Still am."

"Tell me about it," says Wilcox. "But not too many details."

"Remember Willie Fielder? The guy who spied on us, behind the tree?"

"How could I forget? But he forgot, didn't he?"

"Right. After you used The Look on him. Well, he was spying on Suzie Steele and me, behind the gym."

"What were you doing there?"

"I was showing her my new watch." Jerry holds out his arm. "And I . . . gave her a little smooch."

"Oho! So what happened then?"

Jerry scowls. "Willie drew a picture on the blackboard. Of two dogs kissing. He put my initials, and Suzie's, under the dogs. Everybody laughed."

Wilcox smiles. "And what made you so angry?"

"She's my girlfriend! And he's a snoop! He had no right to . . ."

"To do what? Use his eyes?"

"No. It's bad to spy on people."

"Well, it's not very honorable. We'll work on your anger tomorrow. I need to rest now." Wilcox rises to his feet.

"Will you be okay?"

"Yes. I feel better now."

"That's good because . . ." Jerry looks at his watch. "Yikes! It's really late. Mom will kill me!"

"I'll be fine, Jerry. I just need some rest."

"How about food? Have you got something to eat?"

"Not tonight. I might not keep it down. But maybe you could bring me some food in the morning."

"Sure. Tomorrow is Saturday. No school."

FIVE

ON THE right side of Jerry's house, the purple embers of the sunset give the trees an eerie glow. He's all out of breath. His mother is sitting on the front porch with Jade the cat in her lap. The porch light is already on.

"Where have you been, young man?" Then she gasps. "There's blood on your cheek!"

Jerry's still panting. "Just a scratch, Mom. I ran through some brambles. Near the junkyard." He doesn't want to worry her. And he *did* run through some brambles. But did he lie? Wilcox said no lying.

"Be more careful, dear. You could put your eye out."

"Yes, Mom. But I was hurrying. It was so late." That was also true. But was it also a lie?

Now she's looking more closely. "Where did you get that?" She jumps up, dropping Jade, and points to the bump on his head. "It's as big as an egg!"

Jade hisses, arching her back.

Jerry hesitates. Only for a moment, but long enough to seem suspicious. Why didn't he plan what to say? That was so dumb! "I . . . I . . ."

"You poor dear! Come inside." She rushes to the fridge, dumps ice into a dish towel. "Hold this against it."

Good, Jerry thinks. *She's forgotten her question.*

No such luck. "Now tell me *all* about it," she says.

Jerry's mind is writhing with possibilities. He fell. A fight. Some guy threw a rock, and it accidentally . . . He can't tell her the truth, can he? She'll squeal like a stuck pig!

"Jerry! Tell me what happened. Right now." When she uses that tone, you don't dare fib.

"Sit down, Mom. Please."

Her eyes grow wide, but she does.

"Now don't get all panicky, Mom. I'm all right. But a bald man hit me on the head. He tied me up, too."

"Mercy! Who was it? Tell me!" She's jumping around, waving her arms. "How did you escape? How?"

"Take it easy, Mom. I'm okay now. After a while, the bald man left, and I, uh, managed to get free. Then I ran home."

"We've got to call the police. Maybe they can catch him! Wasn't Wilcox at the junkyard?"

"Um, yeah. But at first, he was out." Jerry smiles at his pun. "He's there now."

"With that awful man?"

"No, Mom. Like I said, the man left. He was, um, going on a long trip."

"A trip?" She gives Jerry a long, suspicious look. "There's something you're not telling me. What is it?"

"Nothing, Mom. You can ask Wilcox." Whew! Jerry's glad he thought of that. Wilcox will back him up.

"All right. But I'm going to call the police. I absolutely am. Maybe the bald man didn't really leave. Maybe he'll come back. Anyone who tried to kidnap you would tell lies too."

"No, Mom. I'm sure he meant it. He won't be back."

She gives him another piercing look. "How can you be sure?"

"I just know. You can talk to Wilcox tomorrow. The man hit him too."

"What!" Her eyes grow wide. "He hit Wilcox too?"

"Yes. Even harder than me. But he's all right. I'm gonna take him some food tomorrow." Suddenly, Jerry feels hungry. "Can I have some supper now, Mom? Something smells good."

"Yes, of course, dear. I was keeping it warm. But you scared me so. It's mac and cheese, your favorite. While you're eating, I'll call the police."

Jerry digs in. It's delicious.

His mom's on the phone, getting more and more frustrated. She comes back angrily twisting her apron.

"They say they can't do anything. The bald man could be miles away by now. They need evidence. Got more important things to do, blah blah. Kids tell crazy stories all the time, blah blah. Last week, it was a spaceship from Saturn." She snorts indignantly. "The policeman asked if your bald man had an antenna on his head. I could hear snickering in the background."

Jerry nods. "It's okay now, Mom."

"When I told him Crazy Wilcox could verify your story, he laughed right in my ear." She sips some tea, sighs. "How do you complain about a policeman to the police?"

"I dunno, Mom."

They eat in silence. Jerry can't believe how hungry he is.

His mother works her tea bag like a little yo-yo. "Well, there's nothing wrong with your appetite."

"Thanks, Mom. I'm awful tired now. I need some sleep."

"All right." She plinks down her teacup. "Just leave your plate in the sink. Clara will wash it. You go take a splash in your marble bath."

Jerry smiles weakly. "I'm too old for that joke, Mom."

"Sorry. Your papa used to say he'd rather hear a good joke a hundred times than a bad joke once."

Jerry rolls his eyes. "And please call him Dad, Mom. I'm eleven now."

"Well, excuse me, Mister Shore!" She kisses him on

the forehead. "Get a good rest, honey. And let me know if you need anything. I'll call Dr. Granger tomorrow. It'll be Saturday, but I'll call him at home."

SIX

THE next morning, Jerry tells his mom he doesn't need Dr. Granger. "The swelling's gone way down. I looked in the mirror. And I feel fine." Two out of three are true. "Way down" is a matter of opinion.

She looks skeptical. "Well, all right, dear. You seem okay. But please take it easy. The bump is still there."

"Sure, Mom. I promise. I've got to take Wilcox some food."

Arriving at Denny's Deli, Jerry smiles. When "Denny" retired, a Chinese guy named Mr. Wu bought the place. Below the big sign DENNY'S DELI, he put up a plaque that said: "We Smelly Velly Welly." It was just for laughs, but some of the customers stopped coming, so he took it down.

Jerry buys a quart of milk, a loaf of bread, some sliced turkey, and lettuce. He pays with a twenty-dollar bill. The clerk gives him a long stare, like he might have to identify him later. He must have noticed the bump.

Turning to leave, Jerry almost faints. The store begins to swirl. Coming in the door is the bald man who tied him up!

Wobbling on his feet, Jerry gapes. Same gray beard. Same ears that stick way out. Different clothes, but it's the same man for sure! What should he do? Run? Yell for help?

All this flashes through Jerry's head in an instant. Staring in horror, he drops his bag of groceries, *thunk*, on the floor. Scooping it up, he runs around the man and out the door.

Hurrying along the sidewalk, Jerry checks the bag of groceries. Somehow, the bottle of milk didn't break. Bread must have cushioned it. He wonders: Can a hit on the head cause visions? Is he "seeing things"? But the bald man seemed so real!

Holding the bag like a football, Jerry feels his head. The bump is smaller, but still sore. Is he going crazy? Is this what madness is like? Will he start seeing the bald man around every corner? Even in his dreams?

He frowns to keep from laughing madly.

Before long, he's at the junkyard.

Wilcox is sitting calmly in front of his cardboard house.

Jerry puts the paper bag on the ground beside him. "Here's some food," he says. "I sent him away. He can't be back! Am I crazy?"

Wilcox opens his eyes. "Thank you, Jerry. What happened?"

"At Denny's. The bald man. He was there. I think I'm going bonkers."

Wilcox looks him in the eye. "You seem all right to me," he says.

"But how could he be back? Why didn't The Look work? The man was totally in my power."

Wilcox hesitates. "Maybe you shouldn't think of it that way. It's not about your power. It's about doing the right thing."

Jerry thinks for a minute. "I get it," he says. "Is that what . . . went wrong? Do I need to have pure intentions when I use The Look?"

"It helps." Wilcox gets a dreamy look, like he's entering a trance. After a minute, he snaps his head. "But perhaps you did nothing wrong."

At that moment, they hear a crunching noise. A figure appears between the trees.

"It's him!" Jerry cries. He jumps up, ready to use The Look again.

"Wait!" says Wilcox.

The bald man walks up to Jerry. "Excuse me for following you, son, but you seemed to recognize me. My name is Reginald Foster. My brother Fred is missing. My twin brother. Maybe you've seen him?"

Jerry gapes, but manages to nod.

"We're identical twins, you see. The only difference is the gap in our front teeth. Mine is smaller." He smiles, displaying the smaller gap.

"I'm Sam Wilcox," says Wilcox. "And this is Jerry Shore."

"Please to meet you," the man declares. "I'm afraid my brother is a rather unsavory character. And he's got a screw loose." He twirls a finger beside his ear. "We had someone watching him, but he managed to slip away. I hope he didn't do anything disgraceful?"

"He was going to cut off my fingers," said Jerry.

"What!" The man's jaw drops. "Fred lives in a fantasy world. But he's never harmed anyone." He turns to Wilcox. "Is this true . . . about fingers?"

"I wasn't conscious," says Wilcox. "Your brother knocked both of us out, and Jerry came to before I did."

"Knocked you both out? Oh, I'm so sorry! Are you all right?"

"Evidently," says Wilcox.

"He kept singing Dum de dum," says Jerry.

"Yes, Freddie does that. But he's never been violent before. Something must have snapped. I'm afraid he must be . . . confined. Locked up for safety. Do you know where he is?"

"He went South," Jerry declares. "He plans to walk five miles a day."

"Really? How peculiar. Well, I must hurry. Here's my card." He hands Wilcox a little white card, trimmed in gold. "I'll contact my security service at once. I hope we can keep this a secret. Five miles a day, did you say?"

"Yes." Jerry smiles. "You can count on it." He pictures Fred Foster marching South, like a good soldier. Left, right. Left, right. Dum de dum.

SEVEN

WHEN Reginald Foster is out of sight, Jerry says, "You knew he wasn't the same person, didn't you?"

Wilcox shrugs. "I wasn't sure. But his clothes were very different. I didn't think he'd get all dressed up, just to come back."

Jerry smiles. "Yeah. I was hung up on his face. Those weird ears. I'd like to twist them off."

"Oho!" Wilcox raises his eyebrows. "So you're angry again?"

"He hit both of us! He almost cut off my fingers!"

Wilcox looks sad. "Maybe he couldn't help it."

"What! Anybody can—"

"Not anybody," Wilcox declares. "The man is mentally ill, Jerry."

"Yeah, but . . ."

"I once knew a woman," says Wilcox, "who thought

she was a rainbow trout. She'd stand naked before a full-length mirror, admiring the rainbow sheen that only she could see. And she kept gasping for water. She was only happy when she was swimming. Or taking a bath. People laughed, but she suffered greatly."

"What happened?"

"I cured her with The Look. But I overdid it at first. She wouldn't drink any water, wouldn't even go near it. She was convinced that water would harm her. I had to use The Look three times. I wasn't very good at it yet."

Jerry whistles.

"Her fantasy was very real for her," says Wilcox. "Just as what we see, and touch, seems entirely real to us. She deserved a lot of sympathy. And so does our sick bald friend."

"Sympathy?"

"Yes, and prayers. Severe mental illness can be terrifying."

"He terrified me."

"Yes. But he was probably suffering inside. Reginald said that Fred lives in a fantasy world. In a way, we do too. He's a prisoner of his own perceptions, just like we are. It's just that his perceptions are warped." Wilcox rubs his head. "Dreams are a good example, Jerry. Crazy things happen, and we totally believe them to be true, even though they aren't. Dreams imprison us too, but they are like a short life we often remember."

Jerry thinks this over. He manages to feel some

sympathy for Fred, but he's still upset about his fingers. And about getting hit. And about the man's hitting Wilcox. All of a sudden, he makes a connection. "What about Willie Fielder? Is he a prisoner too?"

"Yes, we all are. But the right path can set us free."

"I know." Jerry nods. "But it's hard."

"It helps to think of karma," says Wilcox. "When people hurt you, they make bad karma. After that, bad things will happen to them. Sooner or later a person's actions, good or bad, come back to them. That's what karma means. So people who do bad things deserve sympathy."

"Yes, but . . ."

"And if you harbor hatred or ill will, you create bad karma *for yourself*. Anger toward someone else harms the person who is angry."

Jerry chews on this for a while. "So I should be nice to Willie?"

"Well, yes, if possible. Kill him with kindness, as they say. "You don't have to love him. Just be kind. Picture Willie as a helpless baby in his crib. Or as a little child. Maybe he just hurt himself . . . or his father hit him."

Jerry's eyes grow wide. "I've heard Willie's father is a drunk. And a gambler. Maybe he did hit him! Maybe he still does."

"See? To know all is to forgive all. Everyone has some hurt, Jerry. And they mistakenly pass it on to others. But if you can truly forgive Fred, and Willie, *deep in your heart*, you will be kinder. And you will create some very good karma for yourself. Especially if you pray for them."

"I will," says Jerry.

"Do it when you meditate, when you feel close to your Higher Self. But don't be proud of doing it. You must *not* let your Ego sneak in. Remember? Down, Ego, down. Good boy! Heel!"

Jerry laughs. "I'll do my best," he says.

EIGHT

THAT night, in his room, Jerry meditates extra long. He peacefully slides, deeper and deeper, into the Silence. Then he prays for the bald man and Willie. It seems to be working fine. He's doing it! He's helping them—and helping himself too!

Uh oh. Jerry feels proud of what he's doing. He can sense his Ego, sneaking in. He quickly thinks "Heel!" but the spell is broken.

The next day is Sunday. The sun shines warm and bright, as if it feels joyful on its name day.

Jerry's mother makes French toast. The bread is a perfect golden brown. Jerry sits at the kitchen table, eating and smacking his lips. He keeps adding more maple syrup, until the sugary bread seems to float.

"Mercy, Jerry! That's too much. You'll waste it."

"No, Mom. I'll lick it all up when I'm done."

"Heavens! You're a hopeless barbarian!"

"I'm not." Jerry holds up a wad of paper napkin. "I'm using this instead of my sleeve."

"Well, praise the Lord." She kisses him on his unscratched cheek.

After breakfast, Jerry checks his bump in the mirror. It's still pretty obvious. He scrapes his hair up over it the best he can. There. Now it's much harder to see. They go to church on foot. The bright sun feels warm in the cool spring air. For some reason, Jerry thinks of a hot fudge sundae. That's weird. Is his brain any different now? Does he make different connections?

At least the bad bald man is far away. What was so scary about his face, anyway? Except for those stick-out ears, he looked pretty normal. The things he said and did must have added scariness to his face.

Sitting in the church, Jerry sees Suzie Steele across the aisle with her parents. She adjusts her bouncy blonde curls, gives him a zingy smile. Is she thinking about the kiss? Jerry hopes so. She hasn't noticed his bump yet. It's pretty well hidden.

Wait. Maybe she's thinking about the cartoon on the blackboard. She was embarrassed at first, but now she doesn't care. Is that what she's thinking? Jerry has a brief, eerie feeling that it is.

Beyond Suzie sits Willie Fielder. His father is asleep already, snoring softly. His wife nudges him awake.

Preacher Plutz snatches at the air. The flies are thick today. Will he snag one? Probably not.

Jerry wonders why he seems to attract them. Maybe he uses some spicy aftershave lotion . . .

What is the sermon about? Jerry hears the word "forgiveness." Maybe he'd better listen. "Turn the other cheek," he hears. Hey, that's pretty funny! Almost like the preacher has noticed Jerry's scratch.

"'Vengeance is mine; I will repay,' saith the Lord." That one gets Jerry thinking.

Preacher Plutz drones on and on. He talks about a lady in a famous book who killed herself, and Jerry flashes on Monty Flowers. Once Monty said he was "thinking about thooithide," and Jerry thought it was a joke, but now he's not so sure. Monty gets teased a lot because of his lisp, but he can't help that, can he? What's he supposed to do, get a new mouth?

Jerry sighs. Monty has great talent for drawing . . . After Jerry pleaded and begged, Monty showed him some cartoons he had drawn. The sketch of Cromer Borkin was a snorting bull, but it still looked exactly like Cromer! Peter Wardly was a snooty-looking rat, dressed like a schoolboy. And there were so many others. Even one of Monty himself, looking like a frightened little mouse.

Amazed by Monty's talent, Jerry had persuaded

the art teacher Mrs. Meer (called Mrs. Smear behind her back) to give Monty free art lessons at her house. In return, Monty promised to give Mrs. Meer ten percent of all the money he makes when he becomes a famous artist.

Jerry smiles, remembering how he convinced her to make the deal. Monty must be a real pro already. His parents are poor. They could never have afforded art lessons for Monty . . .

Rustling, rising noises startle Jerry out of his reverie. People are putting hymnbooks back, standing up to leave. Church is over.

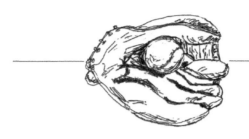

NINE

OUT in the bright sunlight again, Jerry and his mother start walking home. But Suzie looks at him urgently.

"You go on ahead, Mom. I'll catch up soon."

"Why, Jerry? Are you . . . Oh, I get it. All right." She isn't dumb.

Suzie's eyes are wide. "Jerry! Are you okay? You've got a lump on your head!"

"I know. I had an accident."

"What kind of accident? What happened?"

Uh-oh. He hadn't planned on this. "Suzie, uh, promise you won't tell?"

"Sure, Jerry. What?" Her eyes sparkle like twin diamonds. "I won't tell a soul."

Jerry steers her off the sidewalk, behind a clump of bushes. "A bald man hit me on the head," he whispers.

"What!"

"Not so loud, Suzie! It's a secret."

"But are you all right?" she whispers.

"Sure. Just don't tell anyone."

"I won't. But why did he hit you?"

"He wanted money. It was sort of a kidnapping. He tied me to a tree."

"What!?"

"Shush! Not so loud.

"But where is the bald man?"

"I, uh, made him go away."

"How? Weren't you scared?"

"Yeah, a little."

"So how did you escape?"

Uh-oh. He's in deep trouble now, but the adoring look on Suzie's face is worth it. "The man is, uh, mentally sick. It wasn't hard to persuade him to let me go." Jerry breathes easier now. "Then his brother came. He's going to contact the police. They'll catch him. But please don't tell."

"I won't," says Suzie.

"I hear my mom calling me. 'Bye." She gracefully skips away.

Jerry blinks. Off to one side, something moves. Somebody was listening! Who was it? Willie?

He focuses more clearly. It was only a little tree, but he could have sworn it was a person! How could he have thought that?

At supper that evening, Jerry's mother gives him a smug, knowing look. "You like Suzie, don't you?"

"Uh, she's okay." Jerry yawns, but not very convincingly, he fears.

"She's pretty as a china doll."

"Yeah, I guess so."

His mother smiles. "She'll grow up to be a striking beauty. I can tell. Probably marry somebody handsome."

Jerry slams down his fork, startling Jade, curled up on the kitchen counter. The cat likes him, but sometimes he spooks her, and he accidentally threw up on her once.

"Can we talk about something else, Mom? I'm getting my mitt ready for the big game on Tuesday."

"Of course, dear. You're going to play your big rival."

"Right, Mom. The Danville Daggers. They've got a great pitcher. He's already been scouted for pro ball!"

"Mercy! At age eleven?"

"I've heard he's thirteen. He stuck two years. Maybe a little dense, but he's got a wicked curve. Hey! Do you think dumb guys make good pitchers?"

Jerry's mother eyes him over her teacup. "What makes you say that, dear?"

"Peter Wardly's a good pitcher. He's not very bright either." Jerry snickers. "Last year, he didn't know when The War of 1812 happened."

"What?"

"I think he was daydreaming in class, but still. He's not the sharpest thumbtack on the bulletin board."

Jerry's mother smiles. "I really don't think there's any connection, dear. But I'll be cheering for the Lions."

"Thanks, Mom. After *The Shadow*, I'm gonna work on my mitt."

Every Sunday night, Jerry listens to *The Shadow* on the big radio in the living room. Lamont Cranston (The Shadow) can "cloud men's minds" so they can't see him. In tonight's episode, he tweaks and pinches two bad guys until they're fighting each other. Lying on the rug in the dark, Jerry laughs.

Up in his room, Jerry unties his proud possession. He keeps a softball tied tightly in the pocket of his mitt—to keep it perfectly shaped. He plays hardball, of course, but the softball makes the pocket bigger.

He removes the ball, puts on the mitt, punches the pocket with his fist, and grins. This mitt will catch anything!

From the shelf above his desk, he takes down a can of linseed oil. Pouring a few drops in the pocket, he rubs it in slowly, carefully. Then he does the fingers, too. His mitt is famous in the entire sixth grade. Nobody has anything near that perfect. Jerry guards it with his life.

TEN

MONDAY morning, when Jerry walks into class, everyone goes quiet. They stare at him like wooden statues, carved with open mouths.

Then some of the guys rush over.

"Hey, Jerry! You okay?"

"Let's see the bump!"

"Can I feel it?"

"How long were you out?"

"How deep is that cut?"

"Did the bald man really torture you?"

"How did you make him go away?"

"Where is he now?"

"Did the police get him?"

Jerry closes his eyes. Suzie must have blabbed! He glances over. Her pink face is buried in a book.

44

At recess, he corners her. "You promised, Suzie!"

"It's not my fault, Jerry. I only told Eva and Molly. And they both crossed their hearts they wouldn't tell."

Jerry frowns. Eva Ning and Molly Kewel were always whispering secrets.

"Suzie. You knew they'd tell."

"No, I didn't. They both swore to God." She looks at him with pleading eyes. "I'm sorry, Jerry."

"I forgive you," he says.

At recess, Cromer Borkin walks over to Monty Flowers.

Monty cringes like a frightened mouse. He's as small as Cromer is big. Some of the guys close in around them.

"Hey, Monty!" says Cromer in a loud voice. "Geth what I thhee?"

Uh-oh, Jerry thinks. He's mocking Monty's lisp. That means trouble.

"Skeeters!" cries Cromer. "Watch out for the skee-ters!" He slaps Monty on his arm, hard. "They're swarming all over you." Laughing, he swats Monty's shoulder, too.

Monty staggers backwards, but doesn't fall.

Peter Wardly catches on. "Yeah, Monty. Swarms of skeeters. I'll save you!" He slaps Monty on the cheek. "Don't let 'em bite." He whops Monty on the back of the head. "Got one! Hee hee."

Jerry comes over. "What's going on?"

"We're saving Monty from the skeeters. Isn't that right, Monty?" Peter gives him a threatening look.

"Yeth. I geth tho."

Jerry glances at Monty. There's a red mark on his cheek, and a red welt on his arm. But Jerry's no match for Cromer and Peter. "Well, looks like you got 'em all." He quickly turns to Willie Fielder. "Hey, Willie. You wanna use my mitt for the big game?"

The guys gasp. Nobody touches Jerry's mitt!

Willie narrows his eyes. It's a trick for sure, but what's the angle? "Yeah, Jerry. Right after the moon turns blue."

"I mean it, Willie. You'll need it at shortstop if we're gonna win. I'm only in right field. We'll swap."

Willie stares. His family is poor. He's got a cheap mitt, from the five-and-ten. He'd give anything to have a mitt like Jerry's! "What's the catch, Jerry? What do I have to pay?"

"Nothing." Jerry smiles. "Use it for practice today, see if you like it."

Like it! Willie can't believe his ears. Getting hit on the head must have made Jerry crazy! "Thanks, pal." He gives Jerry a warm smile.

Afternoon practice is light, but serious. "I want you guys sharp," says Coach Britton. "Be careful. No stupid injuries. We gotta beat those guys!" He smiles grimly.

Jerry does his best with Willie's flat, flimsy glove.

How does Willie ever use this thing? At first he feels totally awkward, but after a while he figures he can manage.

Then his mind wanders. He shouldn't have doubted The Look. It always worked before, didn't it? He should have trusted it. Still, he wishes he hadn't given his address to the crazy brother Fred, even though he really had no choice. At least, he made him forget it!

Plunk. A fly ball lands beside him in the grass.

"Wake up, Shore!" cries the coach. "That one almost beaned ya!"

ELEVEN

THE big day arrives. It's cloudy and breezy.

Both teams are on the field. The bleachers are already half-full. The band is warming up. Blue and gold banners saying LANGDON LIONS are flapping everywhere.

Jerry wears his cap turned around because it looks cool that way. He watches Danville's ace pitcher warming up. The guy is so big and tall, he looks like a pro already. Jerry's never seen such curve balls! No wonder they call him "Curvy" Crane. He's going to be almost impossible to hit.

As the game begins, Peter Wardly strikes out the first three Danville batters. He's looking good. But can anyone get a hit off "Curvy" Crane?

Willie Fielder is the leadoff batter for Langdon. If

he can just get on base, he's fast as greased lightning! He can steal pitchers blind.

But Willie fans. His wild swings don't even come close. Curvy grins and adjusts his cap.

Next up is Harry Davis, a good hitter. He fans awkwardly too—and smashes his bat into the ground in disgust.

Now it's Jerry's turn. Coach Britton gives his arm a squeeze. "Just a single, Jerry. Just meet the ball. If you get on base, Cromer will knock you in."

Jerry nods. "Right, Coach." Cromer bats cleanup, and he hits a ton of home runs. They even call him "Homer Cromer."

Jerry takes a few warm-up swings. He spits in the dirt, because that's what good batters do. Then he marches confidently up to the plate, even though he's got butterflies in his stomach.

He glances over at the stands. Suzie's eyes are glued on him. She looks like she's holding her breath. Jerry gives her a grim smile.

Curvy adjust his cap, squints, and throws. It's a fastball, coming straight at Jerry's head!

"Duck!" someone yells.

Jerry nimbly backs away, and the ball curves right down . . . over the center of the plate!

"Stee-rike!" yells the umpire.

Jerry stares. How did the ball do that? But he couldn't argue with the call. He steps back in the box, bangs the plate with the tip of his bat for luck.

Curvy squints, throws.

It's another fastball, straight for Jerry's head. He won't be fooled twice. He steps into it . . . and the world disappears.

When Jerry comes to, he's lying in the grass, on one side of the diamond. Coach Britton is bending over him. "Easy, son. He knocked you out. You got a nasty crack."

Suzie stands just behind the coach. Her worried face is twisted with horror. She's fingering her rusty-nail charm, her lips moving silently. *Oh, please. Please, God.*

Did Suzie say that out loud? Jerry has an eerie feeling, like the one he had in church. He tries to smile at her. *I'm all right.* His head is aching and spinning, worse than when the bald man hit him. Fate seems to have singled him out for punishment! Or was it karma? Did he do something in the past to deserve this? He'll have to ask Wilcox to say more about what karma is.

Meanwhile, two teachers carry him on a stretcher to the school nurse.

Much later, Jerry learns what happened. After he was hit by a pitched ball, he was supposed to take first base. But he couldn't, so the coach put Monty Flowers in to run for him. Then Cromer hit a home run, right on schedule! The Langdon Lions won, 2–1. Jerry and Cromer are heroes.

Willie Fielder is a hero too. Using Jerry's mitt, he made four sensational plays to keep the Daggers from scoring.

Dr. Granger declares that Jerry has a mild concussion. He needs plenty of rest. No homework for three days!

Jerry's mother is a flurry of fluffed pillows and kisses and chicken soup. "Couldn't you win the game some other way?" she asks.

"Stop spinning, Mom," he pleads.

Jerry's dizziness stops, but his bandaged head still aches. When he dozes off, he has visions of the bald man, swinging his knife through the air. He tells himself that's impossible. But his stupid brain remembers, and his eyes see these phantoms. He's a prisoner of his perceptions, like Wilcox said.

Fred, the bad bald man, is still walking South—or else the police have picked him up by now. So there's no logical reason to see any visions.

Jerry slowly heals. He meditates for hours, hoping to make contact with his Higher Self. He tries to forgive the bald man and Willie. He's glad that Willie used his mitt to help win the game. He'll probably want to keep it forever now. Well, why not? *Kill him with kindness,* Wilcox said.

TWELVE

IT'S LATE afternoon. Jerry's resting in bed. Jade the cat is curled up near his feet. When Jerry dozes off, he still has scary visions of the bald man with the ears. Jade whines and bares her claws, almost like she understands.

Maybe Jerry's visions aren't because of the hit on his head. Maybe he's a little crazy. Or maybe they're caused by his medicine. Should he stop taking it? He could easily palm the little pills—and flush them away.

His mom sticks her head in the door. "Somebody to see you, dear." She has an incredibly stupid smile on her face.

"Hi Jerry." Suzie takes two cautious steps into the room. Her golden curls jiggle. She looks even prettier because she's blushing. She holds one hand behind her back.

"Uh, hi, Suzie." He gives his mom a hard, go-away look. She disappears, but leaves the door open.

Suzie takes another step. "How do you feel, Jerry?"

"Better *now*," he says, hoping he's not blushing too.

"You look like a handsome pirate." She giggles, pointing at his bandage.

He likes the word handsome.

"I, uh, brought you something." Suzie's hand appears, holding a box wrapped in red happy-birthday paper. "I know it's not your birthday, but . . ."

She comes closer, hands him the box. "I made them myself."

Jerry's hand lands on hers. "Thanks, Suzie."

He holds on, pinning her hand to the box. She doesn't try to pull away! Her hand is warm and soft. He wishes he could kiss her again.

Suzie smiles. "Do you wear your new watch at night?"

Jerry stares. Did she read his mind? "Yes," he manages to say. "Thanks for the gift."

She smiles again. "They're chocolate chip."

"That's nice," says Jerry, still holding on to her hand. *Nice! What a dumb thing to say.*

"Everybody misses you at school," says Suzie.

"That's nice," says Jerry. *Not again! What's wrong with him?*

She finally frees her hand. "I hope you'll be back in class soon."

"I will." Jerry does his best to smile handsomely. "Dr. Granger said maybe next Monday."

"That's wonderful." Suzie nods, jiggling her curls. "I've missed you. Well, 'bye."

Smiling, she twirls and walks gracefully out the door.

Jerry collapses back against the pillows. He spends the next couple of minutes reviewing the dumb things he said. But she's been missing him! That was really good to hear.

He gently shakes his present. It makes a crumbly scraping sound. He strips off the red paper and opens the box. It's filled with chocolate chip cookies, of course.

Jerry pulls one out, takes a bite. It's much too salty and hard as a rock, but he loves it.

After a little while, Jerry's mom is back. "There's a whole bunch of kids outside to see you, Jerry. But I told them no more than two minutes each. You're still a little weak."

"Okay, Mom. Thanks." Weak? After seeing Suzie, he feels strong as a superhero!

In walks Willie Fielder. "Hi, Jerry."

Jerry stares. Has Willie changed? Is he warm and

happy because Jerry loaned him his mitt—or because they won the game?

"Hi," says Jerry. "Thanks for coming."

"I hope you're feeling better."

"Yeah. But it hurt plenty for a while."

Willie fidgets. "I, uh, want to thank you for lending me your mitt. It really helped!"

"Sure, Willie. I heard you stopped a lot of runs, saved the game. Why don't you keep it?"

Willie's eyes grow wide. "Keep it? For good?" Jerry really is crazy now, that's for sure!

"Yeah, why not?"

"Gee, thanks, Jerry! You're a great guy. I had you figured wrong."

Jerry smiles. "You're okay too, Willie. Have a cookie." He holds out the red happy-birthday box.

Willie takes one, bites down on it.

"Like it?"

"Um, yeah. It's, uh, very crunchy."

Jerry's mom sticks her head in the door. "Time's up, Willie."

"Right, Mrs. Shore. Get well soon, Jerry."

Downstairs, Cromer Borkin is next in line. As they pass on the stairs, Willie whispers: "Don't take a cookie. It's a joke. They're dog biscuits."

THIRTEEN

CROMER comes in. Jerry's always amazed at the size of his arms. He could wrestle an alligator! "Hi, Cromer."

"Hi, Jerry. How ya feeling?"

"Better, thanks. I heard you won the game with a home run."

"Well, yeah. But if you hadn't, er, got on base . . . the score would have been one to one." He laughs. "You should have seen Monty when he ran the bases for you. After the ball went over the fence, the little fool took his sweet, stupid time. I had to push him."

Jerry laughs. "He was proud of it, huh?"

"Yeah. I don't think he ever scored before."

"You know," says Jerry, "Monty's not a bad guy."

Cromer's face darkens like a thunderstorm. "That little jerk? I can't stand his stupid lisp!"

At the foot of the bed, Jade hisses, arching her back.

"He can't help it, Cromer."

"He . . ." Cromer thinks about this. "Well, at least he could try."

"No, Cromer. It's the way his mouth is. His mouth makes him lisp, just like your muscles make you strong."

"Yeah? Well, maybe. But I still think . . ."

Jerry's mom comes in. "Time's up," she says. "Sorry."

Peter Wardly is next. "Hello, Jerry."

"Hi, Peter. I heard you pitched a great game."

"Thanks. But Cromer really won it. And Willie made some amazing saves. Your mitt was like magic."

"Yeah. I've really worked on it. I told Willie he could keep it."

"What!" Peter gapes. Is Jerry some kinda psycho now?

"Why not? He uses it better than I do."

"Gosh, Jerry. That's really good of you." He thinks for a second. "Especially after that . . . picture he drew on the board."

"That was just a cartoon. I got over it. Willie was probably just jealous."

"Yeah, probably."

"Sure. Want a cookie?"

Peter hesitates. Willie warned him too. "No thanks, Jerry. I had a snack at Denny's after school."

"Time's up," says Jerry's mom, sticking her head in the door.

After three other kids, it's Monty's turn. He was probably pushed to the end of the line.

"Hi, Jerry. How are you?"

"Monty! I'm better. I heard you scored a run!"

"Yeth. Thankth to Cromer . . . and you."

Jerry notices that when Monty says "Cromer," he shudders. "How's it going with Cromer?" he asks.

Monty frowns. "He's still on me . . . about the skeeters. I've got some pretty bad bruises."

Jerry calmly nods, but feels a wave of anger inside. "I, uh, just talked to Cromer. Maybe he'll forget about the skeeters now. Anyway, I'll be back in school soon. I'll try to help."

Monty smiles. "Thankths, Jerry."

"But if he keeps it up, you can always draw a cartoon of him. Something to make everybody laugh."

Monty's face goes pale. "I wouldn't dare, Jerry! He'd thmash me to thmithereens. Hope you come back thoon." He turns and leaves the room, waving shyly, almost like a girl.

"Thanks for coming, Monty!" Jerry frowns. Monty's a good guy. Why does he act so silly? It's like waving a red flag in front of Cromer!

The next morning, after breakfast, Jerry is reading in the living room when the doorbell rings. Who can it be? All the kids are in school now. It's probably one of

58

his mom's friends, but she's in the bathroom now. She suffers from "constipewshun" and eats a lot of prunes.

"I'll get it!" Jerry calls.

He opens the door, and it's Wilcox!

"Hi, Jerry. How are you feeling?"

"Better, thanks. Come in, please."

They sit in the living room. "I'm using my, uh, vacation to work on anger," says Jerry.

"Excellent. How's it going?"

"I was doing okay until Monty stopped by. Cromer's still on him about skeeters."

"Skeeters?"

"Yeah. Cromer claims they're swarming all over Monty. So he slaps and swats him."

"Oh, *imaginary* mosquitoes. They give Cromer an excuse to hit Monty."

"Right. Other kids do it too."

"That sounds dangerous." Wilcox grimaces. "Bullying is the worst when everyone piles on. The pain really adds up. A few little pebbles aren't so bad, but enough of them can cause an avalanche."

Jerry feels horror prickles. "Monty mentioned suicide once, but I thought he was joking."

"He might have been half-serious, trying it out on you. Please be his friend whenever you can."

"I am. I got Cromer off his back by giving Willie my mitt."

"You gave Willie your mitt . . . permanently?"

"Well, yeah. I lent it to him for the game. He played great, so I said he could keep it. Killed him with kindness, like you said."

"That was a fine thing to do, Jerry. And a good way to distract Cromer. Temporarily, at least. Did Willie appreciate the gift?"

"Sure. Him and me are friends now."

"Your motives are better than your grammar. How do you yourself feel about Willie now?"

"Pretty good. And I'm trying to make my Ego heel."

"Wonderful." Wilcox smiles. "Good morning, Mrs. Shore."

In the doorway, Jerry's mother beams. "Thank you for coming. Would you like some tea or coffee? And there's a piece of apple pie this eating machine couldn't quite devour."

Wilcox laughs. "No, thank you. I got a bite at Denny's. I just stopped by to see how the hero is doing."

The hero! Jerry smiles. "I'm not really a hero." But he likes the sound of the word. And he *was* sort of wounded in action. Maybe Suzie thinks so too.

"Do you mind if we do a little light meditation and prayer, Mrs. Shore?"

Jerry's mother stares. "Why, no. Not at all. I've got some laundry to do."

Jerry grins. His mom is smart.

Wilcox and Jerry just sit quietly. Jerry knows what

to do. Seek the inner Stillness. Try to get in touch with his Higher Self. Somehow, it feels better with Wilcox there.

After about twenty minutes, Wilcox clears his throat. "Now let's briefly focus on Willie and Fred. Let's try to see them both in peaceful light."

They do that for about five minutes.

"Okay," says Wilcox. "Now let's focus on Cromer and Monty. Try to hold them in the peaceful light."

Another five minutes pass.

"Well, that's that." Wilcox stands up, smiling.

"That's all?"

"Well, yes, for now. You're still pretty weak. Do it longer as you heal." He gives Jerry a knowing look. "And as your Ego heels."

"Right." Jerry laughs.

"I made a pun, but I'm serious. Keeping your Ego away from a negative force actually protects you from negativity. If you can, meet hostility with positive forgiveness and active love. This will help you to master your own negative emotions. You won't be burdened with seeking revenge. Both you and any potential enemy will be free of the urge to create bad karma."

"Thanks," says Jerry. "I'll do my best. But I was hoping for a plan of action, when I get back to school."

"Changing your attitude *is* action," says Wilcox. "Praying is powerful action too." He gently squeezes Jerry's shoulder. "Work on forgiving Cromer for picking on Monty. If Cromer lives long enough, he and his powerful muscles will eventually lie helpless on his deathbed. Maybe then, at least, he will realize the pain he has inflicted.

"But if you can forgive Cromer, and help him to understand the harm he is causing, perhaps he will change now. Even if he doesn't appear to change, you'll feel better. When you erase your anger, when you replace it with complete forgiveness, you open a door to the light of your Higher Self. And who knows?

Maybe you'll get an important inspiration, just when you need it."

FOURTEEN

DR. GRANGER gives Jerry the all-clear for school. "But no baseball for three more weeks," he says.

Jerry's mother is delighted. "You're a wonderful doctor!" she tells him. "I really think the boys ought to wear helmets when they bat."

"What a good idea!" says Dr. Granger. "Maybe they will, someday."

Jerry returns to school. Everyone really does treat him like a hero!

But Cromer still picks on Monty, and the other guys still join in. Jerry feels helpless and sad. He tries to treat Cromer with positive forgiveness and active love, but it's not easy.

The teasing, the bullying, seems to feed on itself. The other guys can't resist piling on. And poor Monty just takes it. Day after day! What choice does he have?

Cromer gives Monty hard pinches and knuckle-digs on his arms, making more purple bruises. Monty's parents must think he has a lot of accidents on the playground!

Jerry tries to take Monty's side. But it's hard to stand up for him. It's two against so many! What can he do?

He doesn't seem to feel any inspiration yet. Being a hero is fine for him, but not for Monty. Still, he keeps at it.

And every night, he meditates and prays.

One morning, over scrambled eggs and bacon, Jerry opens up and tells his mom about how Cromer and the other guys bully Monty. She is horrified. "That poor boy!" she gasps. "Let's have him over, cheer him up. I'll make a good dinner, and he can spend the night."

"I'll ask him," says Jerry.

As soon as Monty arrives, Jerry's mom pours cokes from a large bottle into two glasses with ice. She spills a little, handing Monty his glass. "Oops, sorry!"

"Thankth, Mrs. Shore."

"I'm so glad you could come." Her smile almost turns into a giggle. She's been sipping sherry in the kitchen for some time.

From the oven, the thick aroma of a large, bubbling pot roast fills the air. With flowered mitts on both hands, Jerry's mom plunks it down on a metal stand in the center of the table. "That's called a trivet, so the pot won't make a divot." She laughs nervously.

Nobody else laughs at all.

"Mee-ow," says Jade, curled up on the kitchen counter.

They sit down, and Jerry's mother takes another sip of sherry. "It's nice to have you here, Monty."

"Thankth, Mrs. Shore."

She coughs loudly. Jerry wonders if she's covering up a laugh. He told her all about Monty's lisp!

"Have some pot roast, Monty," he says. "It's my mom's specialty."

His mother passes Monty a large spoon. "I think things taste better when they simmer in each other's juices." She smiles. "Try some, please."

"Thankth."

"Why, that's not enough to feed a bird!" She heaps Monty's plate, spilling some of the juice in his lap. "Oh, I'm so sorry."

Jerry rolls his eyes.

"Thath's all right." Monty sops it up with his paper napkin.

"Monty scored a run," says Jerry. "When we beat the Daggers."

"Yes." His mom's eyes are shining. "So I heard."

"Only because I ran for Jerry," says Monty, chewing. "Thith ith delicious."

"Thank you, dear." She takes a long sip. "My own special recipe. "It calls for a dollop of wine, hee hee."

Jerry raises an eyebrow. He's never heard of *that* before.

The conversation lags, but they're busy eating.

Jerry's mom pours herself more sherry. "I wonder where Herky is," she says, her eyes sparkling impishly over her glass.

"Mom!" did you really need to mention that?"

His mother turns to Monty. "Herky was his invisible friend," she confides. "When he was little. Herky had a red nose. And he wore clown clothes."

Jerry frowns. Jade hisses softly.

Monty doesn't know what to say, so he says nothing.

They eat in silence.

Jerry's mother tries again. "Jerry's father knew a man," she says. "He had a company that sold canned salmon, but people wouldn't buy it. The meat was perfectly good. But it was white, not pink. And salmon has to be pink, right?" She sips her sherry. "Well, the man put stickers on the labels: 'No artificial coloring added.' Then people started buying it like crazy, hee hee."

"That's a good one, Mom." Jerry laughs.

"Yeth," says Monty. "That wath clever."

After second helpings, Jerry's mom brings out a chocolate cake. "Fresh from Betty's Bakery," she says. "And there's vanilla or chocolate ice cream." She takes another sip.

Monty and Jerry dig in, and she leans back, smiling.

"It's hard to believe you boys are so grown up. Seems like just yesterday when Jerry was three."

She closes her eyes, purring like Jade. "One time, his father was trying to teach him arithmetic, to get a little jump on school, don't you know."

Jerry yawns. He's heard this one before.

"So his daddy says: 'If I had ten lollipops and gave you three, how many would I have left?' She laughs and sips. "Little Jerry jumps up and says: 'Where are they?'"

Monty smiles. "That wath pretty thmart."

"Yes. Another time, Jerry was impatient to go swimming. His father was finishing up some work, but Jerry kept pestering him. 'We'll go soon,' he said. 'Keep your shirt on.' So when they got to the swimming hole, little Jerry went in wearing his shirt!"

Monty laughs and laughs.

Jerry gives his mom a warning look, but she's just getting warmed up. "Once we went to Harry's Hideaway for dinner. It's called Burger Delight now. They had rough wooden tables, with little cracks on top between the boards." She takes a sip. "Well, Jerry's father secretly pulls out an envelope. He sticks it up through one of the cracks like a little white sail. 'Look, Jerry!' he says, moving it back and forth." She smiles, remembering.

"Well, while Jerry's watching the envelope, *zip*, his father yanks it down out of sight. Little Jerry's mouth drops open. And you should have seen his eyes. As big as two saucers!"

Monty smiles. "Like it wath magic."

Jerry stretches. "Maybe that's enough, Mom. I want to show Monty—"

"One more story," she interrupts. "It's so cute! We were trying to get Jerry toilet trained, see. He'd been using his little potty on the floor. And, to tell the truth, I was tired of cleaning it out.

"Well, he'd sit perched on the big seat, making ploppers, as we called them. But he wanted privacy, so I had to leave the room." She smiles a devilish smile.

Jerry shudders, but there's no stopping her. The house could burn down, and she'd keep right on talking.

"His favorite bath toys were two rubber yellow ducks. Quackie and Jackie, he called them. Well, little Jerry would balance one on each thigh, and make them talk, hee hee. I'd stand just outside the door and listen. It was so cute."

Jerry's glaring at the ceiling, but Monty's fascinated.

"One time, I heard *kerplunk!*—and a little yelp. Jerry had fallen in, and he couldn't get out! I had to hoist him up by his little arms."

Jerry scowls, but his mom and Monty are laughing like mad.

"You boys go play," his mother says. "Clara will clean up the dishes."

"Who?" says Monty.

"Family joke," says Jerry, grabbing him by the arm. "C'mon. Let's go up to my room."

Sitting sideways on Jerry's bed, they talk for a while. "Your momth friendly," says Monty.

"Yeah." Jerry rolls his eyes.

"Laughing made me feel better," Monty declares. "I was pretty sad, with Cromer and the skeeters."

Jerry nods. "I know. I wish we could do something." He pauses. "But if you tell your mom, it might make things worse."

"Yeth. My parents don't understand. They don't even listen to me anymore. Sometimes, I just go off by mythelf and cry." Monty laughs bitterly.

Prickles climb Jerry's spine. The bullying cuts Monty off from everybody! It makes him unbearably lonely.

Jerry secretly clenches his fists. "Where do you go?"

"The thwimming hole. There's an old thiak bethide it."

Jerry nods. The old shack beside the swimming hole. But he doesn't say anything. He's still trying to think up a plan to win Cromer over.

"Time to get ready for bed!" Jerry's mom calls. "It's a school night."

"Okay, Mom!"

Jerry's bed is small. Monty's family is poor, but he's borrowed a sleeping bag from Harry Davis. "Don't get cooties in it!" Harry had said—but he did let Monty borrow it.

FIFTEEN

When Jerry gets home from school the next day, his mom says, "I hope you didn't mind my telling stories on you. I wanted to cheer the poor boy up."

"No, Mom. You were great!" What else can he say?

She sighs. "I paid for it, though. What a headache! I drank too much sherry, trying to seem natural. I didn't want Monty to think it was staged."

"He's better now, Mom, thanks."

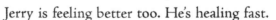

Jerry is feeling better too. He's healing fast.

But that night, he has the scariest dream of his entire life.

He's lying in his bed, in a deep sleep, when someone flicks on the light switch just inside his door. The bare overhead bulb floods the room with cold, white light. Instantly, he's wide-awake.

Slowly and smoothly, the bald man with the ears slips into the room. But he's wearing good clothes! Jerry has a flash of hope. It must be Reginald, the good brother!

The man walks up close. Uh-oh. He's got a gun. He waves it around. He smiles a mean smile. There's a wide gap in his teeth! He's Fred, the bad brother, no doubt about it.

"Hello, you little schmuck. Surprised to see me?" He's pointing the gun directly at Jerry's head.

"Mom!" Jerry yells. "Lock your door! Call the police!"

"Quiet!" The bald man holds out his gun. "She's already tied up and gagged, sonny boy. I tied her to the bedpost. Hope she isn't uncomfortable. Dum de dum."

Jerry's mind is reeling. "How . . . did you get here? You were supposed to be . . ."

"Walking? Don't be silly, schmuck! Your little Look didn't last long. It wore off after a couple of miles. Fortunately, there was a policeman nearby. Who says there's never a cop around when you need one? Haw haw! I knocked him out and borrowed his gun. See?" He waves it menacingly in the air. The barrel flashes in the light.

"But . . . But . . ."

"You tried to make me forget your name, Jerry. And your address. But The Look wore off, so I remembered them." His lips pull back in a sneer, and Jerry can see the large gap again. "Now I need you to tell me where the family riches are."

Jerry stares.

"Riches?"

"Yes. And don't pretend you don't know." He waves the gun again. "Tell me where they are, or . . . we'll see how good this gun is. Dum de dum."

"We . . . We don't have any riches."

"Nice try, schmuck. Your mother denied it, too. Suspiciously, I might add. But I know they exist. Diamonds and rubies and piles of gold! Probably in the safe. Yeah. Where's the safe?"

This guy is really loony! Jerry tries The Look. He stares deeply into the bald man's eyes, thinking the magic word Wilcox taught him.

"I told you, sonny boy. The Look doesn't work anymore. Not that it ever did! Now where's the safe?"

Jerry gulps. "We don't have a safe, either. I think you'd better calm down and—"

There's a sudden, deafening noise. A bullet rips into the plaster above Jerry's head. "No more stalling, schmuck! Tell me where the safe is, or the next bullet finds your hand. Yes, you've got too many fingers. Dum de dum."

Jerry flings away the covers. He leaps to the floor, running wildly . . .

And wakes up back in bed.

The sun is streaming in his window. His hair is

sweaty and cold. His hands are trembling. That dream was so real! Wilcox was right. We really are prisoners of our own perceptions. *Dreams are like a short life we often remember.*

Jerry walks unsteadily to the bathroom and pees. Then he throws on some clothes and goes down to the kitchen.

His mom is standing at the stove. "Good morning, Jerry. I'm glad you got a good rest. I was just about to wake you. I'm making— Jerry! What's wrong? You look like you've seen a ghost. Maybe two ghosts!"

"I . . . I had a bad dream, Mom. A really bad dream." He slumps down onto a chair.

"You poor dear. Want to tell me about it?"

"No."

His mother closes her eyes, lips silently moving. Soon she opens her eyes, cautiously smiles. "Maybe a good breakfast will help. See? I'm making pancakes."

"I'm not hungry."

"You will be, after you taste some." She puts a plate before him with three steaming pancakes. They're a spotted golden brown.

"Thanks, Mom." They do smell pretty good. He slathers butter over them, drowns them in maple syrup.

"It's good to see you eat, dear. You'll feel better soon." She sighs. "Only eleven, and what a life you've lived already! Well, your father used to say that an unlived life isn't worth examining. He liked to play with Plato."

"I think you told me that," says Jerry. He's busy shoveling down six more pancakes.

His mother smiles. "Not bad for somebody who wasn't hungry."

"Thanks, Mom. I do feel better now."

The doorbell rings. "I'll get it!" Jerry jumps up, runs to the front door. He swings it open wide . . . and gasps.

It's the bald man with the ears! For real! It's not a dream. He's completely wide-awake now.

Jerry's body freezes. He can't run or walk or anything. But his mind is whirling.

The man is wearing good clothes, so it's the good brother. But the good brother Reginald didn't know his address. Only Fred did. Wait! How big is the gap in his teeth?

"Smile!" Jerry almost screams. "Smile!"

SIXTEEN

IT'S SPOOKY. The bald man doesn't smile. He just stares at Jerry's face. "Hello, Jerry. I didn't mean to frighten you." As he speaks, his front teeth reveal a small gap!

Jerry's too numb to answer.

"I came to make amends," Reginald Foster declares. "May I please come in?"

"Uh, sure, Mr. Foster."

Now the man smiles. It's definitely a smaller gap! "I got your address from Mr. Wilcox. I offered him some money in compensation for his injury, but he politely refused."

Reginald looks over Jerry's shoulder. "Is your mother home? I'd like to talk with both of you."

"Oh, sure. Hey, Mom! We have a visitor. A friend."

Jerry's mother, wearing an apron, appears. "Hello, Mr. . . . ?"

"Foster. Reginald Foster, Mrs. Shore."

"Sorry I'm not more presentable. I was washing dishes. Come into the living room, please."

"Thank you. My brother Fred, I'm sorry to say, is the one who hit Jerry on the head. I've come to offer my condolences . . . and offer some recompense."

Jerry's mother squints. "The man who went on a long trip? Has he been caught?"

"Yes indeed, my dear lady. And now he's locked up safely in my house with a security man to guard him. Fred has never been dangerous before. I'm so sorry. But I am a man of honor. And a man of means. As I said, I'm here to offer Jerry . . . and you . . . some recompense."

Jerry's mother gives him a proud, haughty look. "Thank you, Mr. Foster, but we don't accept charity."

What? Jerry stares. *I was knocked out! I was tied up and threatened with . . . finger amputation!*

"Wait a minute, Mom." His mind is churning like mad. How can he persuade her? "The, uh, reward money we got from the bank is run-ning out. This isn't really charity either. My head still hurts, and I'm having nightmares. And Mr. Foster really wants to do it. Right, Mr. Foster?"

"I certainly do, my lad. I'm so sorry about the, er, adverse repercussions." From an inner pocket, he slides out a shiny, dark-blue checkbook. "I'm prepared to be quite generous."

Jerry stares. "C'mon, Mom. Please!"

His mother smiles. "Well, I guess one little check wouldn't hurt."

"Excellent!" Reginald produces a gold fountain pen. He scribbles on the top check with a great flourish. "There." Ripping the check away, he hands it to Jerry's mother. "I made this out to Jerry, Mrs. Shore, but I'm sure you'll—"

Fortunately, Jerry's mom is standing near an armchair when she faints. The big chair catches her like a giant softball.

Jerry gently slaps his mother's face. She comes to pretty fast. "Oh, Mr. Foster!" She's still holding the check. "This is too much, really."

Reginald Foster smiles. Same smaller gap. "My pleasure, Mrs. Shore. But I do have a favor to ask. If you're all right now."

"Certainly. Yes of course I am I just . . ." She's still gripping the check, gaping like it's an airmail letter from Venus or Mars.

"I wonder if Jerry could come with me to see Mr. Wilcox. I still want to compensate him, even though he turned my offer down." He pats the pocket that conceals the checkbook. "Maybe Jerry can help persuade him."

Jerry jumps up. "Sure, I'll go with you, Mr. Foster. Are you positive your brother's locked up safe?"

Small-gap smile. "Fred is in my house, locked up tighter than a drum, I assure you. And he shows no signs of hostility."

SEVENTEEN

JERRY and Reginald Foster tramp through the forest.

"This sure is nice of you, Mr. Foster." Jerry smiles. "I'll do my best to persuade Wilcox. But he doesn't care much about money."

"Well, at least I can try," says Reginald Foster.

Off to one side, something moves. Jerry twists his head sharply. Was somebody spying on them? No, it's only a little tree. But didn't that happen before? Where was it?

Wilcox is sitting on the ground as usual. "Good morning, Jerry. Good morning, Reginald. What brings you two here?"

"Mr. Foster still wants to, uh, compensate you," says Jerry. "He gave my mother a very generous check! I really think you—"

"Thank you." Wilcox smiles. "I have everything I need."

"But just a small recompense," says Reginald Foster. "I'd feel so much better." He reaches for his checkbook.

"I understand," says Wilcox. "And thank you again for the offer. But my recompense was how well Jerry handled the situation."

Reginald Foster shrugs. "Well, please accept my apologies once again, for Fred. He's locked up safely in my house, and he seems to be feeling some remorse. His psychiatrist has high hopes." He smiles. "Anyway, you have my card. If you change your mind."

Wilcox shakes his hand. "How is your brother doing?"

"He's calm now, thank you. But we have to feed him his meals. For some reason, he thinks his fingers have disappeared. It's the most peculiar thing! He is unable to dress himself. I won't even mention what happens in the bathroom."

Wilcox gives Jerry a questioning look.

Jerry nods.

"I think maybe I can help with that," says Wilcox. "Can you bring him here tomorrow morning?"

"Certainly. But how will you . . ."

Wilcox smiles. "I'll do it by hypnosis. Jerry was a bit overzealous."

"Really? You mean, he also . . ."

"Yes. But I can undo it. The process will be quite

safe. And I'll try to make sure he doesn't do any more physical harm."

"Thank you. May you both thrive and prosper."

So saying, Mr. Foster crunches away through the forest.

Wilcox turns to Jerry. "Sit down, if you can stay for a while."

Jerry sits.

"What happened with the fingers?" Wilcox asks.

Jerry squirms. "My head felt awful. I was dizzy and angry. He was about to cut off *my* fingers! I wasn't thinking straight. When I used The Look, I told him to cut off his own fingers. But I cancelled that right away. I said forget all about your fingers, or something like that.

Wilcox nods. "Remember your promise to use The Look only for doing good. You must speak with great care when someone is under. They take your words literally, and it's all too easy to harm them. But I think I can override what you did, make him remember his fingers. And even plant some peaceful seeds." He looks at Jerry carefully. "How is your head now?"

"Much better. But I had a terrible nightmare about . . . Fred. And I keep seeing him as I fall asleep. I see other things too. Sometimes a little tree looks like a person, if I see it out of the corner of my eye. A sneaky person. It's like things around me are plotting to be enemies. Is that crazy?"

Wilcox smiles. "No. You have a good imagination, that's all. And you've been through a lot. Did you know that imagination is a kind of memory?"

"What?" Jerry thinks for a minute. "You mean, when I imagine something, I'm really remembering it?"

"Not exactly. Look at it this way. The mind works by association. When you have a nightmare about Fred, it's based on your memory of him. No matter how far your imagination flies, it always has a launching pad. It's the same with the sneaky tree. The weirdest, most far-out ideas you can imagine are formed in relation to a previous perception."

Jerry ponders this. He thinks of wildly shooting stars and comets with fiery tails and hideous aliens in flying saucers. Yes, they're all related to something else he's learned before. He looks at Wilcox. "How come you know so much?"

Wilcox smiles sadly. "I had a great teacher."

"Where is he?"

"My teacher was a she, Jerry. She was Indian. And she died."

"I'm sorry. What was her tribe?" Jerry has studied Indians in school.

"Not an American Indian. Her family was from India." Wilcox sighs. "She seemed to know everything naturally. She was a sage."

"How did she die?"

"Medical science was unable to determine the cause. She was still quite young. Perhaps some very old karma caught up with her." Wilcox wipes a tear from one eye. "I went to see her in the hospital several times. Even though she was dying, she was always more concerned about *my* health. She had great compassion."

Jerry nods.

"So your health is better now?" Wilcox asks.

"Yes, I think so. But my brain seems to work different now, after those hits on the head."

"Different how?"

"It makes strange connections, like the hot sun in cool air . . . and a hot fudge sundae."

Wilcox laughs. "Your brain is always different, Jerry. As you go through life, your experiences add up. You never have exactly the same brain you had two minutes ago. But remember: You are *not* your brain. It is your mind, with the miracle of Consciousness, that makes the magic. And your most inspired ideas are a gift from your Higher Self."

"Wow! So I'd better be good friends with it."

Wilcox smiles. "Exactly."

"Mind and brain," says Jerry. "The difference between the right word and the almost right word is the difference between lightning and a lightning bug."

Wilcox laughs. "Who said that?"

"Mom says my dad used to say it. But Mark Twain said it first. Dad also said there's a big difference between a Venetian blind and a blind Venetian."

Wilcox smiles. "Very clever. But please don't forget: You are not your brain."

"I won't," Jerry promises.

They sit in silence for a while.

"I'm worried about Monty," Jerry says.

"Tell me about it."

"Cromer still picks on him. And the other guys keep joining in. One day, Cromer tried to slip a strong laxative into Monty's chocolate milk, but Monty saw him and didn't drink it. Another time, when Monty lifted the top of his desk, he found a wad of toilet paper. Used toilet paper."

Wilcox frowns. "Did Cromer do that?"

"I don't think so. But he's the leader, and all the guys follow. Somebody slipped in some spiders once. And a snake. Mrs. Flanders screamed and called Haggy the janitor. Monty's afraid to open his desk." Jerry sighs. But the worst thing is Cromer's Club."

"What's that?"

"They're still planning it. Everybody has to join. There's going to be an initiation ceremony."

"What sort of club?"

"Oh, just a guys' club. But here's the bad part. The initiation is going to be on Saturday, deep in the woods. They're going to build a fire . . . and brand everyone's chest with a poker.

"What!"

"Not really, but Monty doesn't know that. Everybody will sit around the fire, blindfolded, with their shirts off. First, Cromer will say some phony magic words like *Hokus Fokus* and *Abra Cadaver*. Then the branding will start. Each guy will fake a scream when it happens. Monty will be the last. He's the only one who gets branded."

"But not really branded?"

"Right, but he'll be blindfolded. Cromer will hold an ice cube against his chest. Willie said that at first, you can't tell the difference between extreme cold and extreme heat."

Wilcox grips Jerry's arm. "That's terrible!" he says. "The shock could trigger a heart attack."

Jerry's eyes widen. "But if I warn him, Cromer will kill me!"

"Not really, Jerry. But if you want to be a true friend, sometimes you must act. I think you'd better warn Monty. Then he could pretend to be fooled."

"Okay, I will."

"Good. Let me know what happens."

EIGHTEEN

THE next day, on the playground, Jerry takes Monty off to one side, behind the monkey bars. "Listen," he says, "about Cromer's Club. At the initiation, they're going to—"

"I don't care," Monty interrupts. "I'm not going to join."

"What?"

"Yeth. I'll tell them I'm not joining. What more can they do to me?"

Jerry smiles with relief. "Not much, I guess."

"Right. So no more worries. No more worries at all." He laughs strangely. Jerry doesn't like the sound of that laugh.

A few minutes later, Monty walks boldly up to Cromer. "I'm not going to join your club," he says, and turns to leave.

"What?" Cromer seizes Monty's arm. "Looks like you've got skeeters all over!" He starts slapping Monty like crazy. Other guys join in.

Jerry can't stand to see it. In desperation, he blurts: "Mighty Cromer, picking on little Monty!"

"Hey, Jerry!" says Cromer, eyes gleaming wildly. "I see skeeters on you now!"

He swats Jerry, and some of the other guys do too.

With two ugly bruises on his arm, Jerry meditates extra long that night. He tries to connect with his Higher Self. He prays for Cromer to ease up. He tries to forgive him. He even prays that Monty will forgive Cromer.

Falling asleep, he sees a crowd of bald men with stick-out ears and hunting knives.

The next day, after school, he goes to Wilcox. He finds him sitting, as usual, before his cardboard house. "Hi, Jerry," he says without opening his eyes.

"How do you know when it's me?"

"The sound of your walking." Wilcox opens his eyes, stretches, smiles. "What brings you here?"

"I think I'm losing it. And Monty needs my help."

"Losing it?"

"Yeah. I keep seeing scary bald men with big ears. As I fall asleep."

Wilcox gives Jerry a careful, compassionate look.

"When you give up conscious control, you must trust your Higher Self. The visions you see are only on the surface. Let go of them. Let them fall away." He smiles. "Go deep into the Silence. Merge with the Stillness. Then you'll have a chance for Divine Grace."

"What's that?" says Jerry.

"A wave of loving energy from your Higher Self. You need to tune in, and let go of the surface." Wilcox smiles again. "Now how does Monty need your help?"

"He refused to join Cromer's Club. I'm afraid he's giving up. The guys won't stop bullying him. And when I try to stop them, they turn on me."

"Stop fighting them," Wilcox advises. "When you meditate, see Monty in healing light. See him forgiving them. And see them changing their attitude towards him."

"Okay, but I've already done most of that."

"Then open your heart and ask for guidance. If you get a chance to help, maybe you'll know what to do."

"I'll try," says Jerry.

"Good. Readiness is all, as the Bard put it."

"Who?"

"Shakespeare," says Wilcox.

NINETEEN

ONE day, at recess, Jerry slicks his hair down in the washroom. He neatly tucks in his shirt, smiles at the mirror. Then he takes out a little blue tube. Picking off a peppermint Life Saver, he quickly chews it up.

Outside in the sun, he walks up to Suzie. "Want to see a secret?"

"Sure, Jerry. What is it?"

"If I told, it wouldn't be a secret, would it?"

"No, but . . ."

"I'll show you behind the gym. C'mon."

Suzie hesitates. "Why there?"

"Privacy. So no one else can see. C'mon, Suzie."

She adjusts her bouncy golden curls. "Well . . ."

"Here's part of the secret," says Jerry, taking her hand. "I got a lot of money for being hit on the head."

"What! How?"

"The brother of the man who did it gave me a check. A very big check." Jerry grins. "So now I can buy things. Would you like a new bracelet?"

"Sure, but . . ."

Jerry pulls her gently by the hand. "C'mon and see my secret. It's really special."

Suzie gives him a look from the corner of her eyes, smiling in a way that leaves him breathless. "Okay."

As they round the corner of the gym, Jerry glances back over his shoulder. No one is following them.

They stop in the shadows, beside the wall.

As if by special request, a long dark cloud slides across the sun, making the day a good deal darker.

Jerry moves over close to Suzie. "I bought a new watch," he whispers, holding out his wrist. "It's got an even cooler luminous dial. And it's also a stopwatch!"

Suzie squints, leaning in close. "It's hard to tell the dif—"

This time, she doesn't resist at all. There's no slap, either.

And Willie's not spying. Jerry gave him a quarter to stay away.

Actually, Jerry could have saved his money. A few minutes before he started kissing Suzie, Cromer whispered something to Willie and Peter. After that, they were glued to Cromer's side.

And now, just as the dark cloud slides across the sun, Cromer grabs Monty by the shirt.

"Won't join my club, huh, pansy?"

Monty says nothing. The dark cloud looks like a hotdog bun, but nobody notices.

"My club's not good enough for ya, huh?"

Monty stares at the ground.

A lot of guys form a circle around them.

Cromer gives Monty a rough shake. "Lissen, fairy. Do you know what miserable means?"

"This is gonna be good," Peter whispers to Willie.

Cromer wheezes through his fat nose. "Say something! Do you know what the word miserable means?"

"Yeth." Monty wonders where Jerry is. He seems to have disappeared! He came to school today, though. Where is he? Monty's panicky eyes scan the playground, but no Jerry.

High in the sky, the hotdog-bun cloud stretches out until it looks like a baseball bat. Again, nobody notices.

Cromer gives Monty another shake. "I'm glad you know. 'Cause that's what I'm gonna make your life. Miserable. Starting right . . . now!" His thick fingers grab Monty's cheek.

"Ouch."

"Does that hurt?"

"Yeth."

"Yes, sir!"

Willie and Peter lean forward. They fold their arms across their chests, as if they're just as tough as Cromer.

"Yeth, thir."

"And stop that stupid lisp, before I break you in half!" Silence.

Cromer pinches the other cheek. "Does this hurt, pansy?"

Silence.

"Answer me, fairy!" His face is a mask of fateful fury.

"I . . . I feel pain."

"Oh, getting clever, huh?" Cromer grins. "What do you call me?"

Monty grimaces. "Thirrr."

"That's better, fag!" He whops the back of Monty's head, hard. "Soon you'll be begging to join my—"

"What's going on?"

Jerry has broken through the circle of guys.

"Oh, hello, pretty boy!" Cromer gives Jerry a thump on the shoulder. "Come to defend your queer-bait friend?"

Fortunately, the bell rings.

Cromer growls. "Don't worry, chumps. I'll get ya tomorrow."

The unnoticed cloud keeps on dissolving and stretching itself thinner. Now it resembles a rifle, with a wisp of smoke curling from the end.

TWENTY

THAT evening, during supper, the phone rings.

Jerry's mother answers it. She gets a puzzled expression on her face. "It's for you, dear. It's Mrs. Flowers."

Jerry picks up the phone. "Hello?"

"Jerry! It's Mrs. Flowers Monty's mother I'm calling because . . ." She starts sobbing.

Jerry listens. More sobbing. "I'm sorry, Mrs. Flowers. I can't hear . . ."

"It's Monty he left a note oh, it's so terrible! He took his father's German Luger pistol. The one he brought back from the War. He says . . . he says . . ." More sobbing.

Jerry shudders. "What, Mrs. Flowers?"

"The note says he can't live with the pain any more. He says don't try to stop me. My mind is made up.

Please call Jerry to say good-bye. He was my only friend."

"Where, Mrs. Flowers? Where is he?"

"I don't know. He doesn't say. My husband called the police but . . ."

Jerry's mind is reeling. Jiggers! Where would Monty go? Where?

"I . . . I think maybe I know, Mrs. Flowers. No time to talk. 'Bye." She starts shouting questions, but he hangs up.

The shack by the swimming hole! The place where Monty went to cry. Jerry should have thought of it right away. It's almost two miles by road, but he can run cross-country.

"Gotta go, Mom! Be back later."

"Wait! What is it, Jerry?"

The screen door slams. "Please be careful!" she yells.

Jerry's running like mad. His legs are pumping. His heart is thumping. He gasps for air, his eyes wet with tears. He's been expecting something like this, though not quite consciously, for a long time.

He dashes down streets, jumps hedges, cuts across lawns. He's really starting to cry now. He flies through neighbors' yards, setting off dogs like barking alarm clocks. His lungs are burning, but he's almost there.

In the twilight, he can see the old shack and the swimming hole. "Monty!" he cries. "Monty!"

No answer.

"Monty! I know you're in there."

Silence. Only the wind and a few crickets chirping. Then, a low voice: "Don't try to sthop me, Jerry."

"Monty! Let's just talk for a minute. You don't want to do this!"

"My mindths made up. Thith gun hath a hair trigger."

"Monty, wait! There's something you ought to know."

Silence.

"Please! Let me tell you." Jerry's mind is racing. He tries to connect with his Higher Self. What can he say to make Monty stop?

"What?"

"It's, uh, Cromer. He wants to tell you something you'll want to hear."

"What?"

"Wait. I'll get him. It's really important! Promise me you'll wait."

"Okay. But make it fathst."

"I will!" Jerry's still out of breath, but he takes off for Cromer's house. Fortunately, it's not far away.

Desperation gives him a second wind.

Soon he's pushing on the doorbell.

Nobody comes. Jerry's gasping for breath, hands on his knees.

He reaches out to press the bell again.

Cromer opens the door. "Jerry. What's up?"

"It's Monty. He's going to kill himself!"

"What!" Cromer gapes. "He won't do it. He's yella."

"No. He really will."

"How?"

"He's got a gun. You've got to help!"

"What can I do? He hates my guts."

Jerry gulps in some air. "Apologize, Cromer. You're the only one . . . who can do it."

"What? You're nuts! I can't stop him."

"Yes, you can. You've hurt him so much! You can stop him, if you say you're sorry." He stares hard at Cromer. "Can you even *imagine* how much Monty suffers, when he's bullied all the time?"

A corner of Cromer's mouth twitches. Only a little, but Jerry sees it. "Can you imagine what it's like to be inside his bruised little body, knowing there is always more torture to come? Please!"

Cromer is squirming now, but still he hesitates.

Jerry pulls desperately at Cromer's arm. "If you don't try to help Monty, you'll be . . . a murderer!"

"What thuh . . ."

"Please, Cromer. Save his life!" Jerry looks him deep in the eyes. He'll use The Look if he has to, but it's better if Cromer sounds natural . . .

"All right, I'll try. Where is he?"

When they get to the shack, they're both out of breath.

Jerry thinks of his Higher Self. Then he calls out: "Monty! Cromer's here to tell you something. You've got to listen!"

"Okay. I'll lithen. But thtay back. I've got thumthing to do." His voice is shaking. Sounds like he's barely holding on.

Jerry looks at Cromer. "Now," he whispers.

Cromer thinks for a moment. "Hey, Monty. I'm sorry. I'm sorry I've been picking on you. It was really bad of me. I apologize."

Silence.

"So don't do anything stupid, okay? I'll be your friend from now on. I promise!" Cromer looks at Jerry. "That good enough?" he whispers.

In the evening silence, the shot sounds very loud. The bullet shatters the glass of the shack's lone window.

It's amazing what can flash through your mind in a brief instant. Jerry stands there frozen, thinking of Monty's wonderful ability to draw, his terrible lisp, the way everyone teased him so long, never stopping . . .

"Nooo!" Jerry dashes to the shack, flings open the door.

It's dark inside, but he can make out Monty, sitting on the floor.

"I was stharting to put the gun down," he says. "I told you it had a hair trigger." His jaw is shaking. "I wath hurting tho much." He starts to cry.

"Oh, Monty!" Jerry gives him a big hug. He's crying too.

Cromer comes in the door, wide-eyed. Deep in his heart, something wrenches.

Before long, they're all three hugging and crying like idiots.

"I meant what I said, Monty," Cromer whispers. "I'll be your friend from now on."

Acknowledgments

WITHOUT the kind inspiration of Paul Cash, this book would never have been written. My wife Eleanor provided some helpful advice. Of course, they bear no responsibility for any of the story's foibles or failings. That is mine alone.

Also in this series

Jerry's Magic (2014)